Found Lake

Brian Kludt

with RaeAnne Marie Scargall

Illustrated by Spenser Bower

ISBN-13: 978-1957351-16-2

BISAC Codes:

YAF000000 **YOUNG ADULT FICTION** / General

YAF011000 **YOUNG ADULT FICTION** / Coming of Age

YAF005000 **YOUNG ADULT FICTION** / Biographical

Kludt, Brian
Found Lake
Contributing Author: RaeAnne Marie Scargall
Illustrations: Spenser Bower
Editor: Reji Laberje

Interior and Cover Layout: Michael Nicloy

Published by Nico 11 Publishing & Design
www.nico11publishing.com

Be well read.

Quantity order requests can be emailed to:
mike@nico11publishing.com

Table of Contents

To Granny:

Thank for you for teaching me to be me:
Nothing more, nothing less.

Found Lake

Prologue

Some things about the woods never changed. Everything else in the world—shoes, friends, the weather—was always changing, it seemed, but not the forest. The moss always grew on the same side of the thin, white birch trees, and the owls still called out at their favorite dark hours. The red clay in the soil still peeked out along the gravel roadsides. This is what kept bringing Brian back, even after all these years.

Standing in front of the giant living room window of his family's lake house, Brian watched the sunrise on another summer day in northern Wisconsin. Gazing at the orange glow of the early morning, he could hear his grandmother's voice in his mind. He heard her whenever he returned to this place. When he closed his eyes, he could still see her tiny frame, her bright white head of curly hair. He could still feel how warm and comforting her silence was. Since she'd passed away, he always felt closer to her when he traveled back up to the Northwoods.

Brian's wife quietly joined him at the window. He put an arm around her shoulders. He could smell the coffee that was brewing.

After a moment of silence, their children thundered through the room, announcing their outdoor activities before disappearing outside. Brian smiled, remembering when he was their age and how fresh and promising the air of the Northwoods smelled early in the day.

Brian's wife went to pour the coffee, leaving him once more with his thoughts.

Closing his eyes again, his grandmother's voice repeated in his head, "You will always have yourself; you always have the woods." He missed Granny Jane and her cottage, but he would never lose her, because he would always have their Found Lake.

Chapter One

Finally, it was summer!

Brian burst out of the glass doors of his school. The sun instantly hurt his eyes and he loved the way it felt. The school year was over...he'd made it through seventh grade. His mind raced; what would he do first? Throw away all the papers in his backpack? Explore new streets in town on his bike? His smile grew into a giant grin when he decided that, of course, a bowl of ice cream would be his first activity of the summer.

He jogged across the grass, waved goodbye to some friends, and only looked back once to see the school building disappearing behind him. As the sun continued to warm his cheeks, he sighed with relief. No more homework!

It was only a fifteen-minute walk back to his house, but today it felt like hours. He could already taste the chocolate ice cream and the cold metal spoon. He couldn't put one foot in front of the other quickly enough.

As he turned the corner onto Maple Street, Brian saw his house and his dad's car in the driveway. *He's home early from work to congratulate me on finishing the school year!* Brian thought. He picked up his feet and started running around the house to the back door.

"Dad, I'm home!" Brian called out as he came in through the screen door. He paused after a few steps into the kitchen. It sounded like the house was empty, even though he knew his dad was home.

He dropped his backpack on the kitchen counter and called out, "Dad?"

After another moment of silence, he heard a soft voice from the living room. "Brian, I'm in here."

With his excitement returning to his feet, Brian hurried through the doorway and into the living room. He found his father sitting on the couch, alone, staring at the floor. Brian paused yet again. His stomach clenched. Something didn't feel right.

"Dad, school's out. It's summer," Brian said, the smile returning to his face.

Dad still didn't look up at him. His eyes were stuck on a spot on the hardwood floor. His hands were tightly folded together.

Then Dad cleared his throat. "Brian, I have to talk with you about something."

Brian bit down on his lip as he noticed how

red his father's eyes were. In his dad's clenched hands was a crumpled tissue.

"What...what's going on?" Brian murmured.

"Sit down," Dad said.

Brian slowly moved across the room and lowered himself onto the couch next to his father. A tear rolled down the side of Dad's face. The quiet made Brian's ears ring. His stomach hurt even more now. For the first time in his life, Brian was seeing his father cry.

"Brian," Dad began quietly, "I'm sorry if I surprised you. I don't want you to worry, okay? Everything is going to be fine."

Brian started gripping his hands together, too, just like his dad.

"I want to apologize that your mother and I have been fighting so much lately," Dad continued. "We didn't mean to upset you, but..." he coughed, "your mother and I have a lot of things we're not agreeing on anymore. And we've tried to work things out..."

Brian's head joined his stomach in spinning. What was happening?

His dad rubbed his eyes. "Brian, your mother and I...we're going to have to live apart now. We've decided...the best thing is to get a divorce."

Brian froze. He suddenly felt sweat on the back of his neck. His throat was so tight he could barely breathe. The room felt so bright but dark at the same time.

"Everything is going to be fine," his dad repeated.

Brian felt himself shaking his head. *No,* he thought. *No, no, no.*

"Your mother and I still love each other. We're still your mom and dad. We're just going to live in different places now. You'll still see both of us just as much," Dad continued, whispering.

Brian was still shaking his head. Through his closed throat he managed to say, "No. Dad, no."

"Everything is going to be fine," his father said again. Brian didn't believe him—if everything was going to be okay, why was he crying so much?

Where was Brian going to live? Was Dad moving out? Would he have to change schools or move somewhere new?

Brian realized his cheeks were wet and there were tears on his button-up shirt. He was so dizzy. He wasn't in the mood for ice cream anymore. He wasn't in the mood for anything. He almost wanted to be back at school.

Dad set one of his shaky hands on top of Brian's and continued speaking. "I know that you're on summer break now. I've spoken with your grandmother, and you're going to spend the summer with her."

Brian yelped. "Grandmother? The one who lives up north? What?"

"Things here need to settle down a little bit,

and it's best for you to be in a calm place so you can enjoy your summer," Dad explained.

Brian squeezed his eyes shut. He pulled his hands away from his father. "I don't want to leave! I barely know her!"

Dad paused, set his hand on Brian's shoulder for a moment, and then stood up. "It's not good for you to be here while Mom and I sort things out. Your grandmother is being very kind and inviting you for the summer."

Brian opened his eyes again, praying he was imagining this.

He was still on the couch.

His parents were still getting divorced.

He was still being sent away for the whole summer with a person and a place he barely knew.

Dad turned to him once more and said, "Everything will be fine. Please pack tonight, because we're taking you up north tomorrow."

"Dad," Brian whimpered, "where exactly does Grandma live?"

Walking out of the living room and to the back door, Dad said, "You'll be living at Found Lake this summer."

Chapter Two

Nauseous and tired, Brian stared at the hot pavement under his white sneakers. Beside his shoes sat a small suitcase filled with his clothes and case of baseball cards. Cars drove by, but the parking lot he stood in was mostly empty.

Dad was next to him, one of his hands on the car hood. They were waiting for Grandmother.

Brian and his father hadn't spoken much since they'd sat in the living room together the evening before. Brian didn't really know what to say; his head was still whirling. He'd only gotten a few minutes to say goodbye to Mom, and she seemed to be in the same state Dad was. Brian hadn't even called half of his friends.

His father looked away from the road for a moment and said, "You know that I love you, Brian. Promise me you'll let me know when you get up north, okay?"

Brian nodded slowly. He was already homesick for a home that no longer existed. What was home even going to be like when he got back?

Just then, a bright blue car rumbled up to them. Brian stared at its tires, and then slowly raised his eyes. He nearly jumped. The smallest woman he'd ever seen with the curliest hair he'd ever seen was staring straight at him from the passenger's seat. She didn't move a centimeter. The back of his neck started sweating again.

"Brian, this is Uncle Phil," Dad said, gesturing to the gentleman appearing from the driver's seat. "Say, 'Hello.'"

Brian hesitantly raised a few fingers in an attempt to wave. Uncle Phil gave a small smile from behind a thick mustache.

The tiny woman in the passenger's seat had not looked away from Brian for a second. He blinked, the heat of the sun and her stare making his eyes water.

"And this is your grandmother," Dad said. He opened the Cadillac's door, the only thing protecting Brian from that unstoppable glare.

Brian raised his palm in salutation. Grandmother said nothing and didn't move. He'd only met this woman once when he was much younger, and he didn't remember her being like a stone figurine.

Dad grabbed Brian's suitcase and Uncle Phil helped him put it in the back of the car. Brian focused on his sneakers again, afraid to look back up at Grandma. Dad and Uncle Phil spoke quietly with each other and exchanged a handshake.

Before Brian realized it, Dad pulled him in for a tight hug and whispered, "I love you," and suddenly Brian was in the backseat of that growling car—right behind his glaring grandmother.

As they pulled out of the parking lot and began heading north, Brian put his hand against the window to give one last farewell to his father. Dad raised his hand in return, standing with heavy shoulders as the car grumbled away.

For a long time, Brian, his Uncle Phil, and his grandmother sat in silence. Brian felt the unsettling in his stomach worsen with each mile. He counted the passing houses, then fields, then bigger and bigger trees. The landscape was growing less and less familiar, much like the feelings tightening his chest.

Uncle Phil turned on the radio. The jarring voice crackling the speakers made the cramped vehicle even smaller. Brian still had sweat on the back of his neck, even though the air conditioning was blowing. He was in a cage, moving at seventy miles per hour. He clenched his fists. *The least they can do is open the windows!* It was the beginning of his summer, and it seemed that everything and everyone were keeping him from even enjoying the weather.

The man on the radio loudly relayed baseball statistics. Grandmother remained motionless. Brian would sneak glances at the back of her very curly head, wondering if he'd hear her voice that summer—or if she even had a voice at all.

As the trees blended into wooded groves and then unending forests, the murmur of the tires on the highway made Brian's eyes heavy. He hadn't slept the night before. He'd never realized how exhausting uncertainty, disorientation, anger, questioning could be. He somehow found himself drifting off to sleep—and into an unknown summer.

«§»

The Cadillac slid and skid over rocks and dirt as it stopped, shaking Brian awake. The radio had gone silent. Trying to remember where he was and why, Brian slowly lifted his eyes.

The cottage was almost the same color as the soil surrounding it: a deep reddish brown, like the clay pots his mother filled with flowers on their porch in the spring. The cottage's windows were framed in white wood, and the glass reflected the late afternoon sunlight. Dozens of pine trees with long, drooping needles circled the house.

"This is it," Uncle Phil mumbled, breaking

Brian's daze. "Home sweet home."

Suddenly, his grandmother moved for the first time since the car had swept Brian up and away from his home. She swung open her car door, hopped out, and scurried to the vehicle's trunk. Mesmerized, Brian watched her curly head and little hands pop open the trunk door to grab his suitcase and yank it out. She shuffled, the luggage almost as big as she was, to a screen porch on the side of the cabin. She vanished inside.

Uncle Phil turned to look directly at Brian from behind his mustache and flannel-tucked belly for the first time the entire journey. "Okay, little guy. We're here. You enjoy your summer, now."

Brian slid out of the back seat. Pine needles and cones cracked under his sneakers. The Cadillac hummed back to life and, with a quick wave, Uncle Phil was gone.

Brian stood in the same spot for a few moments. He swiveled his head around to take everything in. He was too afraid to move anything else.

The porch door slammed. Brian turned to see his grandmother standing on the porch steps, staring at him yet again.

The mere fifteen feet of dirt and rocks between them was closer to fifteen miles.

He had no idea how much time passed as each of them sized the other one up. His grandmother was tiny, yes, but she stood strong like one of the old pine trees in the yard.

Suddenly, a noise like a purring bear escaped her little mouth. "In."

"...What?" Brian managed.

"In! Inside," she repeated. Then, while frowning at his feet, she yelled, "And get the hell out of my garden!" With that, she was gone behind the porch door again.

Brian gaped. She could speak!

He swallowed, unsure if he had actually just been invited into the cottage or not. After taking one last glance around the pines, he tiptoed to the screen porch door.

The porch smelled of stale cigarettes and mildew. Continuing to tiptoe, Brian made his way to what appeared to be a door to the kitchen. It creaked when he pushed it open, and once he found himself inside the house, he immediately fled for whichever room held his suitcase (and hopefully a place to hide).

Somehow, Brian found that very room without his grandmother spotting him again. It was a small, slanted space with one window on the back wall. There sat his suitcase in the middle, right beside a pole with bright red and yellow stripes spiraling from the floor up to the low ceiling. He thought of the candy canes he'd found in his stocking on many Christmases.

Setting himself on the bed in the corner, he sighed. The room felt comfortingly like home already, but it hadn't made his stomachache go away. He slid the small door closed, retreated back to the bed, and pulled his baseball cards out of his luggage. He'd found his bedroom—no, his fort, his hideaway.

He sorted through the cards, having already memorized the many faces of the players. He thought about his dad sitting on the couch the evening before. He closed his eyes.

«§»

Brian bolted awake to pounding on his bedroom door. A card was stuck to his cheek, and he brushed it off, panicked. He quickly gathered the other cards in his hands and attempted to pile them neatly on the rusty pink nightstand beside the bed.

The pounding suddenly stopped, and the little door scooted open. Brian was once again facing the stare of his grandmother. He shrank into the wall behind him.

Grandma's growl came from the doorway, "We are going to have to make the best of this arrangement."

Brian glued his eyes to his knees, silent.

"We have a whole summer together," she continued, unflinching, "and we can either be miserable or learn to get along with each other."

She paused. The silence made her seem so much larger than she actually was.

"It's your choice. You can come down when you're ready to make that decision."

Brian's face felt hot. He blinked hard.

"Dinner will be ready in an hour," was her final grumble, and she hunched away down the stairs.

Brian's muscles held him frozen for a while.

With his eyes still on his knees, he listened to his breathing mix with the sound of clanging pots and pans downstairs.

How was he going to survive this summer?

He couldn't tell if the gurgling in his belly was hunger or his stomachache announcing that it hadn't left. The smells from the kitchen had already turned his head once or twice, but eating seemed impossible.

Rubbing his thumb into his pant leg, Brian thought about what his parents were eating for dinner that night. Were they eating at their dining room table together? Would they ever eat together again?

Somehow, Brian snapped himself out of his daze and started moving his limbs. Down the stairs, bit by bit, he neared the table where his grandmother sat, already halfway done with her dinner. The room was lit by a single metal fixture hanging over the table.

He sat in front of his plate of goulash, not yet looking up. Grandma chewed quickly and quietly. She was all the way across the table, but her gaze was right on top of him.

The kitchen smelled of her cooking and the small flames smoking in the sitting room's fireplace. He picked up his fork and stared at it, holding his head up with his palm.

By the time Brian finally looked up, Grandmother and her plate had disappeared from the table. She clanged and banged things around in the sink, closed cabinets, and shuffled toward the fireplace. He poked his goulash, nudging some onions to the plate's corner.

The smell of the fireplace vanished behind a cloud cigarette smoke. Brian wrinkled his nose and set down his fork in defeat. The stomachache had won, and his grandmother's smoking definitely helped it.

He lifted his head from his palm. He glanced in the direction of her little shape in the armchair closest to the hearth. *If I run as fast as I can, maybe she won't see me go up the stairs*, he thought.

Brian abandoned his plate. He committed to his escape plan, but he didn't make it past the first step.

Once he'd reached that first step, something caught his eye in the sitting room. It wasn't the fire, the withered furniture, or even the floating gray smoke. Behind her cigarette, his grandma was crying.

Her face was so wet it shined orange from the fire. Her shoulders trembled. For the first time since that morning, Grandma wasn't glaring at Brian—her eyes were closed, she sighed, and her face hung in sadness.

Brian couldn't look away; he couldn't move.

Brian found his jaw dropping. He'd never seen so many adults cry in such a short amount of time. His palms and neck began to sweat again, but it didn't feel the same as it did that morning or the day before. He still felt the ache in his head and belly...but now, someone else was feeling it, too.

Grandma cleared her throat and Brian jumped. "I..." she croaked. "I don't understand it."

For a second, even though the words came from her, a little growly bear, Brian thought he was listening to himself think.

"I just do not understand it...your parents," she lifted a small hand to wipe her cheek.

The room felt suddenly warmer—and it wasn't just the fire. Did she really feel the same way he did? Was she really just as confused? And scared?

She trembled a bit more. A stone figurine couldn't sigh and shiver.

He inched toward the chair next to hers, touched the arm, and sank into the cushion. A log in the fireplace shifted down closer to the embers.

"I never wanted this for you. And I'm so sorry," her voice was quiet.

Brian found himself asking, "Never wanted what for me?"

"Your parents...divorce. It's not fair to you. I never wanted this to happen to you."

I didn't want this to happen, either, Brian thought.

"I prayed you wouldn't go through what your father went through," she continued, her eyes now watching the fire.

Brian blinked a few times, unsure. "How... what do you mean?"

"Your grandpa and I divorced when your dad was about your age. Just like your parents are doing now."

The weight of her words pushed Brian down deeper into his chair.

A few more tears reached Grandma's chin.

Brian didn't quite understand everything she was saying, but he didn't feel quite as lonely anymore.

Grandma turned and snubbed out her cigarette in a glass ashtray beside her chair. She settled back a bit and sighed, "But, here we are. Playing the cards we've all been dealt."

Still unsure of what to say, Brian watched the fire. His thoughts went back to his parents, to his dad. He wondered if Dad had felt this way... this fear of knowing only that everything was changing.

"We better get some rest," Grandma said. "We get up early here at the lake."

Brian hesitated, but wanted to obey. He rose from his chair and stepped toward the stairs.

Grandma lit another cigarette, and although

she herself looked tired, she made no move toward her own bedroom. Exhaling smoke, she said, "See you in the morning."

Brian made it three steps up and turned. "Goodnight, Grandma."

"Granny," she said. A firm but warm smile appeared on her lips in the dark. "I'm your Granny Jane."

Chapter Three

The sun had just started rising when Granny Jane started banging. Brian pulled down his quilt and squinted at the glow coming through his only window. The clanging, slamming, and thumping of Granny's breakfast routine would become very familiar to him throughout that summer.

He sat up, stretched his arms, and noticed that his stomachache was gone, except for some hunger pangs. The mustiness of the cottage still surprised his nose. Tired as he was, he knew there was no sleeping through the marching band coming from downstairs.

Cigarette smoke greeted him as he walked down the stairs. Granny Jane was muttering to herself in her bear purr as a tiny radio hummed on the kitchen counter. Her curly head bounced up and down as she tossed pots and shuffled plates and newspapers.

Noticing him without looking up from her tasks, she grunted, "Morning."

Brian blinked. "Hi."

He stood there for a while and watched her terrorize the dishes. He was too scared to ask for a piece of toast, so he turned to the back door.

Once outside, Brian closed the screen door gently behind him as to not disturb the quiet that Granny was already scaring off. The yard was still cool from the night with dampness collected on the grass and pine needles. He turned his head toward the smell of water and mud.

He followed his nose down toward the lake, catching his first glance at the slightly sloping hill and the pier.

The sun suddenly peaked above the tops of the pines, and Found Lake glimmered. Brian stopped, rubbed his eyes, and opened them again to the expanse of water reflecting the morning sky. Cattails and lily pads stretched far into the ripples from the lake's edges. Everything felt still, but the water seemed to dance as he approached it.

He made his way down to the pier. The moment his sneakers mounted the wood, a wallowing cry echoed over the lake. A black loon with its white-striped neck was saying goodnight and good morning at the same time.

In the brightening sunlight, Brian noticed

something tied to the end of the dock. The rippling water swayed the tall grass and cattails as he neared a small blue boat attached by a single rope to a metal pole. The boat had a tiny motor on its rear and, even though it wasn't running, Brian smelled grease and oil in the air.

There was a bench at the end of the pier, too. He touched it with the tips of his fingers, careful to avoid splinters from the wood that had felt a lot of rain over the years. After looking back up at the cottage for a moment, he sat down on the bench and looked out at the lake again.

The air was warming up already. A fish splashed along the edge of the cattails. Brian's foot bounced at the thought of fishing—and fishing on a boat, no less!

He scooted off the bench and bent down to dip his fingers in the water for the first time. He shivered a bit and wiped his hand on his pants. It was chilly but silky, too. A pan fish looked up at him from under the water before diving deeper into the green weeds.

He lost track of time sitting on the bench, listening to the water and birds. Had his dad sat there, too? Had he caught fish or found secret trails around the lake?

Brian didn't feel homesickness while gazing over the water, even though his parents were still in the back of his mind.

He studied the shoreline for trees with strong

sticks for making a fishing pole. Maybe Granny had fishing poles...would she let him use one? He itched the side of his face, a little nervous at the thought of asking her.

Realizing he might be late for breakfast, he stood up from the bench and shuffled his feet back up the dock. He climbed the hill and the red cottage came into sight yet again. He couldn't hear any clanging or banging, so perhaps Granny Jane had calmed her fury.

Upon entering the kitchen, he saw a plate of eggs and bacon placed in front of the seat at the table which was, apparently, now permanently his. Granny was nowhere to be found, but there was a plate of food in front of her seat, too.

He sat down, feeling in the pit of his stomach how truly hungry he was after avoiding his goulash the night before. He couldn't help himself, and began devouring the scrambled eggs.

The next time he looked up, Granny was watching him from her seat. He jumped, some eggs spilling out of his mouth and onto his lap. She smiled—something he'd only seen her do once, just the night before—and slowly chewed on a piece of bacon.

"So," she started. "What does the lake have planned for you today?"

He rubbed the toes of his sneakers together under the table.

"I...I don't know." he replied.

"Enjoy a day of exploring," she said, clearing her throat. "Tomorrow the work begins."

He watched her watching him, and he couldn't tell if she was smiling because he was now her summertime slave, or if she was teasing him.

"The lake..." Brian started, swallowing the bits of eggs that hadn't fallen out of his mouth, "the lake is pretty cool looking."

"That it is." Granny Jane nodded.

There was still a gruffness in her voice, but Brian was continuing to feel more and more comfortable in her presence...especially after seeing her cry the night before. He felt closer to her and didn't quite know why.

After properly scooping and swallowing another bite of eggs, Brian found more courage and asked, "Do you fish on the lake?"

"I do from time to time, yes." she replied.

"Oh. Neat." Brian wiped the corner of his mouth.

Silence took over the kitchen again. Brian finished his eggs. Granny Jane attacked the sink once more to toss around and wash the breakfast dishes; she then disappeared into another part of the cottage to attend to a different task.

Feeling full and happily without a stomachache, Brian decided to go back outside and take his grandmother's advice. What *did* Found Lake have planned for him? What was out in those woods and on that cattail-covered shoreline?

«§»

It was useless—there was no way Brian was going to be able to save his shoes now.

Looking down at his feet, his brand new summer sneakers had turned from glowing white to sopping wet sludge brown. Bugs buzzed about his ears, and he sighed as he swatted them away. Trudging through the lakeshore's mud, his first excursion around the water already felt like a bust.

Yes, he'd found a few sturdy sticks and cattails to make a fishing pole with. Unfortunately, that didn't really seem to make up for the fact that the lake was sucking and swallowing up his legs, greedily trying to steal his favorite footwear.

It was nearly midday already. His pace around the lake had been so muddy and slow that he'd barely made any distance. He turned, the sun burning his cheeks, and realized he could still see the cottage.

Defeated, he turned (with lots of wobbling and flailing arms) and headed back in the direction of the cottage.

Sharp birdcalls followed him on his wet journey back. He got himself back onto the dock and rinsed his shoes in the water. *If mom could see this right now, she'd kill me*, Brian winced, scrubbing at the layers of soil with his palms.

The shoe rescue wasn't terribly successful. By the time he'd exhausted himself with the washing, he leaned back on the bench and put his arm over his face to block the heat of the afternoon sun. The shoes were still slightly brown, but more wet than anything else.

He found himself using the last bits of his energy to trek up the hill for water. He entered the cottage after setting his wet sneakers on the porch steps to dry. Digging through his suitcase, he sighed with relief that he'd brought an old worn pair of high-top sneakers, too. First lesson learned at Found Lake: fancy, cool clothes didn't make you successful—or an efficient adventurer.

Granny was still hard at work on something in another room. After tying his shoes, he snuck back downstairs.

As Brian leaned on the kitchen sink, chugging a few glassfuls of water, an odd sensation came over him. He'd been alone for almost the entire day so far. Granny didn't go with him exploring or ask him where he was planning on going. In fact, she'd encouraged him to do it all on his own.

He'd never been able to decide what *he* wanted to do with an afternoon before without needing his mom's or dad's permission. Gazing at the hardwood floor, he felt some butterflies between his ribs. It felt good to make his own decisions and not have to be followed by his parents. There was a thrill in knowing that, most likely, his mother would *not* "approve of this situation" (as Brian had heard her say many times over).

Brian turned and looked out the window above the kitchen sink. He took notice for the first time of a shed a bit behind the tree line in the yard. Its roof was the same color red as the cottage, but its walls were made from long logs that looked like tree trunks.

Without disturbing Granny upstairs, Brian snuck out to the shed and, as he approached it, he realized it was more like a small barn. He peeked around the side and saw what looked like a wooden boat and some matching paddles.

Brian pushed open the door and got a face full of cobwebs. He batted them away and squinted in the dusty darkness. *If I were Granny, where would I hide fishing line and bobbers?* he thought.

He gently moved things around—old stacks of newspapers, rusty tools—and tripped on a rake before he located a small spool of clear fishing line with a bent hook tied to the end. He brushed off three layers of soot and dust and slid it into his pocket. He looked around for something resembling a tackle box or a fishing pole, but couldn't find anything.

He exited the shed as secretly as he'd entered it. He felt a jolt of energy shoot down to his feet—maybe it was still going to be an okay summer, after all—and he ran down to the pier where he'd left his fishing sticks. Within moments he had a length of line with the hook tied to the end of a thick cattail. He used the butt of the stick to dig in the dirt for a worm. After a few minutes, and after bending down and dirtying his hands in the soil, Brian nabbed a thin worm.

He tossed the line out into the water from the edge of the dock. Relaxing his excited breathing, he sat down to wait for a fish.

The sun had gotten a bit lower in the sky at this point, but it was still very warm. Brian tilted his head up to the clouds, being careful to not look away from the fishing line for too long.

He wondered what his friends were doing on their first days of summer. Ben had probably gotten his new bike already...Tyler probably had all the guys over at his house, that very moment, drawing the plans for the fort they were going to put in his backyard tree.

He wondered if his sheets would still smell the same when he got home. Would he still have the same bedroom, or live at that same house?

Blinking hard, he forced himself to focus on the line and the birds calling. He set down his cattail fishing pole, pulled off his old sneakers, and dipped his toes into the water.

For the second time that day, Brian completely lost track of time staring out at Found Lake.

Suddenly, the pole bounced, and then bounced again. Ripples circled around the fishing line. Brian was instantly at the ready.

After one more bounce, he pulled up on the cattail pole once. A second passed. Then the pole bounced again. Brian bit his lip, his eyes wide.

There was one last brief pause, and then the fish took off. The line flew out toward the deeper water, and Brian yanked straight up on his bending, strained cattail pole. He grabbed the line with his hand, starting to pull it toward him.

The fish fought chaotically. Zigging and zagging, left and right, the fish battled Brian's grip on the line. Using his other hand, he started pulling the hook closer and closer to the surface, until the top of the water bubbled and out exploded a massive walleye.

Brian yelped. "Holy crap!"

The walleye, a wiggling, wild, muscled fish, flew back and forth, its mouth gaping. Brian saw the hook was right on the tip of its lip—and it looked like it was slipping.

"No!" Brian grabbed at the line faster, trying to swing the fish up onto the pier. And then it was gone.

"Agh!" he cried. He searched the water, grabbing at his hair. How could he lose such an amazing fish?! He stared at the hook, now empty of both worm *and* walleye.

He groaned. That was the biggest fish he'd ever seen. And he'd lost it!

His hands balled into fists, he stared at the still-rippling water. He couldn't believe it. His mom and dad would've been amazed—Granny Jane might even have cooked it for them and congratulated him.

He finally accepted the fish was gone and released a heavy sigh. He dipped his feet deeper into the water. He'd try to catch it again.

He looked up and noticed the sun was nearing the tops of the pine trees. Grabbing his cattail pole and his old sneakers, he made his way up to the cottage to see if he could find something to eat—and Granny.

Second lesson learned at Found Lake: some battles weren't won right away.

Chapter Four

Brian was jolted out of a dead sleep by a blinding light in his eyes and Granny's gruff voice in his ear.

"C'mon," she barked, waving her flashlight. "If you're going to have any success fishing, you need to find night crawlers."

Brian rubbed his squinting eyes and asked, "Granny, what time is it?"

"Midnight. Perfect time for crawlers. Get a move on."

She scuttled down the stairs after tossing another flashlight onto the bed for Brian to use. He stared at it in the dark for a moment, and then mustered the strength to work his legs.

He met her outside in the front lawn among the pines. The stars seemed almost as bright as Granny's flashlight.

She hurried off ahead of him as he struggled to turn on his flashlight. "Down to the lake," she called. "Let's go!"

Apparently Granny Jane had really taken his almost-epic-fish story to heart. He shook his head, and following the beam from his flashlight, trailed her down the hill toward the lake.

When he caught up to her, she was already hunched over and digging about the dirt with her hands. He noticed the old rusted coffee can sitting in the grass next to her.

"Get diggin'!" she grumbled.

Brian squatted down near her, tucking his flashlight between his shoulder and cheek the way she had, and began pulling up soil.

"Here we go," Granny brushed dirt off of two huge squirming night crawlers. She tossed them into the can.

Brian had to dig quite a bit longer than Granny had before he found some bait. The first worm he found, though, was the biggest he'd ever seen. Its pointed pink head wriggled about his fingers. He proudly (and sleepily) showed his catch to Granny.

"That'll get that walleye for you, no doubt," she said.

How does she have so much energy this late at night? Brian thought as she threw clumps of dirt through the air.

They dug about for what seemed like hours in Brian's groggy head. After ten night crawlers he lost count, but he knew he would probably be catching more fish than he'd imagined.

Granny started mumbling under her breath a bit, breaking the quiet. Brian glanced over at her.

"You know," she said, still rather quietly, "Life's funny. You and your father, same age during the divorce, and all."

Brian stopped digging.

"Odd coincidence." she concluded.

Brian opened his mouth again, but nothing came out. He closed his mouth, but then tried again. "Was...was my dad upset when—"

"Yes." Granny cut him off. "Very upset, at first. But he's resilient, just like you seem to be. He found his way. Just like you will."

"Resilient? What does that mean?" asked Brian.

"It means you're tough. You bounce back... it means you can overcome tough times and become even stronger."

A little smile crossed Brian's face. He couldn't remember ever being called "resilient" before. He liked it, though.

The two of them resumed digging for a little bit. They both tossed one more crawler into the old can, and then Granny sighed, "All right, with this many worms you'll have to fish for the next ten years. Let's pack up."

Brian brushed his hands off on his pajamas and shined his flashlight back up the hill. Granny was moving much slower on the return to the cottage. He stayed in step with her all the way to the porch door, and then he opened it for her.

"Thank you, young man," she said and went up inside.

Granny set the can of worms inside the refrigerator after covering it with aluminum foil. She rinsed her hands in the kitchen sink, and then motioned for Brian to do the same.

He turned around after drying his hands to say goodnight, but Granny had already disappeared up the stairs. Remembering how exhausted he was (and now wincing from his reddening sunburn), he made his way upstairs, as well.

Brian watched the pool of moonlight on his bedroom floor as he fell asleep, wondering what his grandmother had in store for the next day.

«§»

Brian's eyes flew open, the harsh late-morning sunlight stirring him awake. He opened one eye. Where was Granny Jane's dishware war cry from downstairs? The cottage was completely silent.

He sat up. He patted at a clump of his hair that stood straight up to the slanting ceiling. *What time is it?*

Remembering the worm-digging excursion

he'd taken with Granny the night before, he grunted. It was far past dawn, and definitely far past the best early fishing of the day.

Thundering down the stairs in shorts and his beaten sneakers, he craned his neck about the house to find Granny. She was nowhere to be found, but...in the corner of the sitting room, leaning against an armchair, was a shining wooden fishing rod.

Once again, Brian found himself gaping. The past few days had been nothing but surprises— both bad and good.

He cradled the fishing pole in his hands. The handle was smooth, pale cork, and the rod was the exact earthy red of the cottage. Had Granny Jane left this for him? He felt nervous touching it, but he found himself holding on tighter and tighter the longer he admired it.

The only thing the rod was missing was bait on its hook; it had been completely strung and was ready to cast, its red and white bobber shining. It was beautiful.

Brian gingerly set the fishing rod back against the armchair and bolted to the refrigerator to grab the night crawler can. He was already sweating with the anticipation of catching that walleye as he blew back into the sitting room, snatched the rod, and tore through the back porch to get to the lake.

When he opened the back screen door, he

stood face-to-face with Granny Jane.

The sweat of excitement on his skin iced over in fear of Granny seeing him with this beautiful fishing pole that was not at all his. On top of that, he'd slept in embarrassingly late.

"Good afternoon," Granny Jane smirked.

Brian's face instantly started tingling with heat under that sweat. Words started clambering out of his mouth: "I...then overslept, well...and, found...pole, tried to..."

"What in the hell are you trying to say, boy?" Granny hollered, the smirk still there.

"I..." Brian took a breath, "I accidentally overslept. I'm sorry. I found this fishing pole... can I...may I use it to fish?"

"It's yours." Granny grinned. "But you're not fishing today. No, sir. You'll have to wait to take that beauty to the lake."

Brian felt the smile burst and then instantly fade from his face. "Not today?" he couldn't keep the disappointment out of his voice.

"Today we're going to the Battleground," Granny Jane said, her fists planted on her hipbones.

"The what?" Brian groaned.

Granny directed him to go put away the crawlers and fishing pole and meet her back in the yard. "And grab those pairs of waders on the back porch on your way out," she snapped in conclusion.

Brian dragged his feet back into the house, his head hung lowly. It physically hurt him to dislodge that gorgeous fishing pole from his hand. Why did they need waders? Battleground? Had his grandmother gone crazy?

Waders in hand, Brian slouched his way back outside.

"Follow me." Granny said. He obeyed.

They made their way through some pines and then the earth became much softer, muddier. It smelled like a bog. Brian noticed a swamp—no, a very dirty shallow creek—up ahead.

"That's Mud Creek," Granny said. "It connects Found Lake to Mud Lake. Look at the trees."

Brian gazed up and around, not really noticing anything special about the trees. He was grimacing at the smell and the still-lingering change of plans for his day.

"They're dying. The trees are dying. Can you guess why?" she asked.

"No idea," Brian sighed.

"The beavers. The darn beavers. They keep building their dams here in this river, and the water floods into the soil...the trees are drowning."

Brian felt water entering his shoes.

"I think it's about time that you and I do something about it." Granny declared.

"What are we going to do?" Brian asked.

Granny slid into her waders (they nearly

swallowed her whole), and turned to face the dam. She waded deeper into the water, and then climbed up onto the dam itself. "It's time to get these beavers out of here."

Brian stepped into his own waders, and looked around for beavers. They were nowhere to be seen. Granny had already started yanking sticks and bits out of the top of the dam and throwing them toward Brian.

"Take 'em and get 'em out of here. Toward the house," she hollered. Brian couldn't tell if she was excited or angry—or both.

And so began the war—Granny, perched like a gargoyle atop the dam, flinging small logs and twigs, and Brian, plodding back and forth, creating piles of dismantled dam pieces.

It wasn't long before Granny Jane's face was red from the afternoon sun and sweaty from the heat. Brian was damp inside of his waders, more from sweat than the swamp.

As they trudged, tossed, lumbered, and dripped with sweat, Granny began explaining more of her theory on the evil of the beavers.

"Our trees can't die out like this," she muttered. "It's our forest. It's our home. We can't let them destroy our home."

After a few hours, after Brian passed the point of extreme thirst and frustration, he found he had developed a system. He'd organize the wooden bits Granny threw his way to make them easier to carry. They could use some of the better pieces for fires.

As the sun began beating down harder, Brian noticed his grandmother's pace slowing. She had stopped, breathing heavily, her forearm wiping the sweat from her face.

Brian waddled through the sludge and water, making his way up onto the dam with his grandma.

"Wanna trade places for a while, Granny?" he asked.

"Yes. Thank you, young man."

He held her hand as she stepped off the dam, and then she made her way out of the water and back to the mud. Brian began tearing and pulling at the logs and sticks, quickly realizing how exhausting it really was.

Within the next hour or so, they had removed only a fraction of the barricade, but water was starting to trickle through like a normal river.

"Look, Granny, water's coming through!" Brian cried.

"About time," she grunted, breaking a long stick in two across her knee.

Another hour passed, a little more water was flowing, and Granny and Brian were unbearably thirsty.

They trudged out of the bog, out of their waders, and hurried into the cottage for water. They stood in the kitchen, watching each other guzzle their glasses, only stopping to gulp air once or twice.

"We should take canteens when we go to the Battleground, Granny," Brian exhaled, setting his empty glass on the counter.

"Good plan of attack," she replied between swallows.

Somehow they found the strength (after a few more glasses of water and olive loaf sandwiches) to return to the Battleground for more. By the time evening arrived and their endeavor ended for the day, almost half of the river was flowing freely toward the lake. Brian could already see some of the soil around the trees drying in the late sunshine.

"That should show them," Granny sighed, moving another load of sticks to the giant pile they'd made. "Let's get more of these back toward the house."

From the top of the dismembered dam, Brian straightened his back and gazed around at their work. He smiled. He was hot, exhausted, and more sunburned than he was the day before—but he shared in Granny's sense of accomplishment.

"Yep, that'll show 'em," he said, his hands on his hips just like his grandmother's.

«§»

After dinner, Brian found himself sitting out on a wicker chair on the porch beside his grandmother. There was a small, cracked wooden table between their seats. She'd brought out the radio from the kitchen, and they listened to a crackling voice relay a baseball game.

The sun was beyond the trees now, and crickets hummed from the yard. Between the radio's buzzing and Granny's complaints about missed swings, loons wailed from Found Lake.

During a commercial break, Granny disappeared into the house. She returned shortly with a tall (and very full) martini glass. Granny took two sips, and Brian immediately noticed the piney smell of juniper and alcohol. She lit a cigarette.

Exhaling, she murmured, "Home sweet home. There's nothing like the woods."

Brian looked through the screened porch and out over the yard. Fireflies had begun floating amongst the tree's trunks.

"Ever been to a big city?" Granny Jane asked suddenly.

"It's not so bad."

"Bah," she barked. "Cities are horrid. Just awful. Can't even see the sky past buildings that tall. It's unnatural."

Brian looked over at her, the gin martini once again at her lips.

"People aren't meant to be cooped up in all that steel and concrete. Ya need fresh air."

"I like it out here," Brian said.

"So do I." she sighed, smoke pluming out of her nose.

"Is it hard living up here alone all the time?" Brian played with a small jackknife he'd found on the table.

"No. I wouldn't have it any other way. I ain't going anywhere."

Brian was surprised that someone like Granny could even see a drop of "resilience" in someone like him. She was the toughest thing he'd ever seen. She'd probably have been down at that river today, waging war on the beavers, whether he'd been there or not.

"Do you ever get lonely?" Brian asked.

She laughed. "I've got Cat."

"Cat?"

As if it'd been waiting for that cue to make its entrance, a massive gray feline loped onto the porch. It paused to look up at Brian for a moment, then glanced over at Granny's smoke rings, and sat down to lick a front paw. Its fur was wild and long, its eyes golden.

"That's Cat," Granny grunted.

"Hello, Cat," Brian said. He wondered where an animal of this size was able to hide for so long without his noticing it.

"She's pregnant," Granny added.

"I did think she was pretty fat," Brian raised his eyebrows. Granny laughed sharply, flicking her cigarette ash into a shallow dish on the table.

As the baseball game crackled on, Granny refilled her martini a few more times and struck many more matches for many more cigarettes.

"Are we going back to war tomorrow?" Brian asked, his thoughts having returned to the beautiful fishing pole waiting for him in the sitting room.

"First thing in the morning," she replied.

He tried to hide it, but Brian's shoulders slumped. The thought of having to wait longer to fish was torture.

Granny was wearing her grin again as she watched him from the corner of her eye. "You'll get that walleye soon enough, don't worry."

The two watched Cat continue licking her paws and roll her swollen belly about the worn carpet.

"You know," Granny Jane said, some of the gruffness gone from her voice, "most people would probably get lonely, living the way I do."

Brian flicked open the corkscrew from the pocket jackknife in his hands.

"Most people might be lonely here, yes. But I fought too hard to keep my woods," Granny repeated, her eyes wandering across the now-dark tree line. "I guess I shouldn't be too bent out of shape about your father and mother. I went through that three times, you know."

Once again, Brian was unexpectedly gaping.

"Yeah, I know," Granny's cackle shot out once more. She sipped her drink and continued, "I just learned that I couldn't quite figure it out."

A hot bolt of anger shot down Brian's back, and the yard echoed his voice loudly for the first time. "But when you get married it's...important. You have to try to work things out. What about everyone else? How are they supposed to feel? What am *I* supposed to do?"

Granny clenched her jaw, turned her head just slightly away from Brian, and inhaled, "Sometimes people have to make difficult decisions. Sometimes those decisions can hurt other people. But here's what I want you to understand: you get to decide what's next."

Brian struggled to understand. "What do you mean, I get to decide what's next?"

"What happens to you doesn't have any power over you unless you let it. Sometimes people go their whole lives thinking that life is tough on them and it holds them down. They blame people who have hurt them and they never move forward. But you are resilient. You will find your path and take it, no matter what happens to you. That's resiliency. No matter what hits you, you just get stronger. It's not what happens to you that matters; it's how you *respond* to what happens to you."

She paused briefly, then added, "Your dad had a hard time with your grandpa and I splitting up, but he was resilient, just like you."

The crickets and green, sweet lake air held the two still for a spell. The breeze had almost completely dissipated.

Brian felt his spit of anger calming; he was beginning to understand everything that Granny said, why she said it. Nonetheless, the thought of his parents' divorce still burned in his mind and the back of his eyes. They were giving up and it was wrong. It had to be wrong. How could it be okay when the very idea of it split Brian's chest in two?

"I know it must hurt," Granny broke his confused concentration, "but your father and mother both love you dearly. This is not because of you, or anything you did. They are two people, two different people, but they still see the good in each other. That's why they had you."

The sunburn on Brian's cheeks appreciated the cool of the tears that were falling from his eyelids. The spit of anger was totally gone, and Brian realized that just sadness was left over.

"It's okay," Granny said. "Sometimes you just gotta let it out."

Feeling the grip of everything (yet still self-conscious), Brian covered his face with his hands. He wondered how long it would take for these feelings to go away. Would he experience this internal tearing and burning every time he saw his parents?

"Will it always feel this bad?" he asked Granny.

"In some ways it will always hurt," she replied gently, "but it will get better with time; it'll get easier. I promise. Just remember how resilient you are. Remember, don't hold on to the past too hard, or it will keep you locked up. Look to the future and follow your heart."

Brian wiped his face and chuckled a little bit. He still didn't feel resilient, but he did like hearing Granny say it.

They sat for a while, the radio transmission becoming white noise in the background. Cat was sitting up again, her eyes still on them. The tip of her tail flicked back and forth.

Granny took a last sip out of her glass, snubbed out her cigarette, and sighed. "Well, the Battleground won't clear itself tomorrow morning. We should hit the hay."

"Okay," Brian said. He truly agreed. His body ached.

Granny reached over and gave the top of his hand a few heavy pats. "You get some sleep, and don't worry yourself so much. You've always got Found Lake."

Chapter Five

Brian awoke to the first war of the day: Granny versus the dishes. The sun was just starting to rise. Cat had found her way to the foot of Brian's bed during the night and was in a fuzzy gray ball on the quilt.

He trotted down the stairs, still sore from the day before, but ready to step onto the Battleground once more.

As he plopped himself down in his chair at the kitchen table, Granny hollered, "Mornin'," through the racket.

She set a plate of scrambled eggs and bacon in front of him.

"Thank you, Granny," he snatched up his fork.

"My pleasure. We'll get at those beavers right away today so you can get your hands on that fishing pole. What do you say?"

Brian grinned. "That sounds great."

Squinting through the bright early morning sunlight, Brian approached the second war of the day: the Beaver Dam Battleground. As they had done the day before, they jumped into their waders and organized a plan of attack. They reorganized their piles, how often they moved them, and who should start atop the dam.

Brian waded over to the dam and groaned, "You've gotta be kidding me!"

"What? What is it?" Granny barked.

"The beavers...the dam...it's almost completely repaired!"

"Good grief almighty," Granny snapped. "It only took them one night? Unbelievable. Just unbelievable."

Brian was gaping, yet again. He couldn't believe these little swimming creatures had been able to replace that many sticks in one single night!

"They definitely didn't get as much sleep as we did last night," Granny muttered, having waded up behind Brian to take a look for herself. "That's just...unbelievable."

The two stared at the work they would have to do—again—and just looking at it made their backs hurt.

"Well, the beavers didn't sit and stare, did they?" Granny growled. "Let's get a move on."

The turmoil of yanking, breaking, pulling, and straining that had begun the day before started once again. Brian worked harder than he had the day before, frustrated and still in shock.

As he tossed long sticks over in Granny's direction, he reminded himself of the second lesson he'd learned at Found Lake. *Some battles aren't won right away.*

"At least it's not quite as hot this morning as it was yesterday," Brian called over to Granny, trying to get her to smile. It was going to take more than that to get that grin on her face this morning—she didn't respond to him at all, grunting every time she snapped a stick on her knee.

They worked in silence for the first few hours. Every now and again, Brian would hear snippets of Granny complaining to herself under her breath, but he could never make out exactly what she was saying. Knowing their progress would be reversed by the beavers that coming night, they moved and worked faster and harder.

"Granny, can you please toss me my water canteen?" Brian asked a while later, throwing a bundle of five smaller sticks her way.

She tossed it up to him and he caught it. He drank, looked up at the noontime sun, and brushed some dirt off of his forehead.

They switched spots. Granny's self-muttering became more audible once she was on top of the dam.

"Gonna try and rebuild in one night, huh?"

she growled. "We'll show you."

Brian tried to cover the smile spreading across his face. Granny was so determined! Who'd ever thought that beavers, of all the animals on the planet, would be players in a massive war.

"World War Beaver," Brian said.

"You got that right," she snipped.

Two hours later, they had dislodged almost three quarters of the dam, and the water was moving much faster and easier than it had when they finished the day before.

The two of them stood back near the trees and watched the water rushing and gurgling. They sipped on their water canteens.

"Well, let's see what the little jerks think of *that*." Granny said. "They ain't gonna be able to fix that up so quickly."

"I wonder if they'll call in reinforcements," Brian smirked as much as his face allowed with the sunburn.

"We can take 'em," Granny hissed, pulling her legs out of her waders.

They walked back to the cottage to drink more water and enjoy a late lunch.

Seated on the screen porch and watching a pair of chipmunks scurry about the yard, the two nibbled on the corners of their sandwiches.

"I think it's time you get out on that lake and catch your walleye," Granny said, sounding a little less tired and irritable than she had before.

Brian looked at her, praying she wasn't teasing him. "I can go fishing this afternoon?"

"You better use the birch canoe," she said.

"The canoe?"

"It's not hard to get it down to the lake. It's alongside the shed."

Brian had a flashback to the other day when he secretly stole fishing line from the shed. "Oh, okay."

"My bet is that your walleye will bite more in the evening, but we can get you out there soon."

Any fatigue he felt from the Battleground adventure that morning had completely disappeared. "I can't wait!" he burst.

Granny cackled. "Just finish your lunch, boy."

«§»

The birch canoe was even more beautiful turned over with the sunlight bouncing off its grain. As much as their arms and backs ached, Granny and Brian dragged the hefty vessel through the yard and down the slope to the lake.

They pushed the canoe halfway into the water on the right side of the dock, and then Brian grabbed the fishing rod and can of worms from the grass and loaded them into the boat.

Granny Jane straightened up and placed her fists on her hips again. "You have your canteen?"

Brian nodded and pulled it out of the back pocket of his shorts. "Yep."

Granny handed him a paddle.

"Where...where should I find a life jacket?" Brian asked, realizing his mother would be hysterical if he stepped into a boat without one.

"Can you swim?" Granny asked.

"Yes. I take swimming lessons at home every summer with my friends."

"Then no, you don't need to find a life jacket. Don't have any, anyhow."

Brian caught himself before his jaw dropped this time, having become used to being surprised by his Granny Jane.

They stood for a moment, Brian's palms growing sweaty with excitement.

"What are you waiting for?" Granny barked. "Get your fish!"

The paddle slid in and out of the lake water with ease. The lake was already warmer than it had been the day he arrived. Left side, dip, pull; right side, dip, pull. Droplets and little bits of algae fell from the paddle every time he switched it from side to side.

Once Brian had cleared the lush field of lily pads, a slight breeze caught his hair. An eagle glided past above and perched itself in a tall pine on the water's edge to watch him. The air was sweet, wet, and fresh, and even though his cheeks were burned, being on the lake soothed and refreshed him.

Gazing at the eagle for a moment, then scanning his eyes across the expanse of the lake, he set the paddle across his knees. He looked back toward the dock. He had made pretty good distance; the cracked bench was a dot on the lakeshore.

Tucking the paddle down into the boat, Brian took in a deep breath. He was ready.

As delicately as possible, Brian lifted the perfect deep red rod and loosened the line. Digging through the can, he found a mighty crawler and put it on the hook. He turned to look back at the pier one last time to see if Granny was in sight, but she had disappeared, yet again, probably to rage war on another project around the farm.

Brian swooshed his arm, pole at the ready, and cast over ten feet from the side of the canoe. The shiny bobber bounced at the surface of the water for a moment, and then things went quiet again as Brian adjusted in his seat. Now it was time to wait.

The breeze shimmered across the top of the water. The bobber danced and then settled again. Brian slipped off his old sneakers. His wooden vessel remained level, even when he shifted about inside of it. He felt like a master fisherman. No walleye was safe from him with that pole and that perfect boat.

He smiled to himself while watching the bobber. Starting to daydream, he imagined the jealous looks on his friends' faces when he would relay this amazing tale to them. They'd never believe it. As hard as the past week had been, Brian could definitely appreciate how lucky he was in that moment. Maybe he'd never go home.

Even though it wasn't evening yet—not prime fishing time—Brian felt that luck would remain on his side. He imagined the grin on Granny's face when he'd return to shore with their freshly caught dinner for the night!

Breaking his wandering thoughts, the bobber began jumping up and down. It wasn't the breeze this time.

Brian was at the ready. His feet were squared, his back straight, his eyes glued. He wouldn't fail this time. He quietly turned the reel a bit, bringing the bobber just an inch closer to the canoe.

After a pause and held breath, Brian saw the bobber dip under the surface of the water. And then again.

He reeled in again, just a bit, and then the bobber dove and did not come back up.

"Gotcha!" Brian cried out, reeling in as quickly and powerfully as he could. The fish fought the line, the bobber still completely submerged. He had it!

The top of the fishing pole bent as Brian reeled and reeled, in, in, in, and he could see the bobber swinging about under the water as it came closer.

It was finally time to grab the line, and Brian braced the fishing pole between his knees. Grabbing the line, he yanked it up.

A fat bluegill flopped around on the hook.

"Ugh," Brian sighed. "A bluegill?"

The fish's mouth gulped and its eye watched Brian.

"Well," he said, "at least you're a *big* bluegill."

Brian carefully removed the hook from the fish's mouth and put it into the wire cage he'd found tucked under his seat. After tying the cage to the front of the canoe with rope, he lowered it into the water to keep the fish alive while he continued fishing.

It wasn't the epic walleye, but it was a start. He wouldn't give up that easily.

For the next three hours, Brian reeled in pan fish after pan fish. He tossed back the little ones, but did manage to snag three husky ones. He realized the sun was sinking lower and lower toward the pines. Brian accepted that his first day on the lake was going to go down in history as "Bluegill Day." This was not going to be the day he would brag to his friends about.

One of the pan fish was about six inches, and he rolled his eyes, knowing that wasn't a very impressive trophy to show off to Granny.

Once he returned to the shore, barefoot, he hopped into the shallow water to slide the nose of the canoe up onto the mud. Collecting his supplies and his catches of the day, he wandered back up to the cottage.

Granny was waiting for him in her wicker chair on the porch.

"Let's see him!" she hooted before he even got the screen door open.

Brian didn't say anything. He held up the wire cage, displaying his three pan fish to her.

Her sharp laughter went on much longer than Brian appreciated. The embarrassment flushed across his face from under the sunburn.

When her giggles subsided, he exclaimed, "This one's at least six inches!"

"Oh, boy!" she cackled. "We'll eat like kings tonight!"

Brian rolled his eyes again and walked into the kitchen. He put the fish in the sink. He'd help Granny Jane clean them once his face was less red and he'd had a glass of water.

He turned around and Granny was already standing there in front of him.

"You gonna get those taken care of?" she asked, her face back to stoic.

"I will later," Brian muttered.

"Absolutely not," she snapped. "You don't let those poor things suffocate in that sink. We clean them now and respect them."

Brian batted his eyes and looked at the floor for a moment, realizing that Granny was scolding him.

She dug around in a drawer for a long, heavy knife and a cutting board. He watched her carefully and swiftly slice open each bluegill, scrape the insides clean to expose their translucent meat, and remove their heads.

"Now then," she said, wiping her just-washed hands on a dishtowel. "You put these lovely fish on a covered plate in the fridge, and we'll start our dinner in a bit."

Brian did as he was told.

Granny disappeared to the porch again, and he went upstairs to change into a T-shirt that didn't smell like fish and lake water.

Before no time, Granny and Brian were back on the porch, plates of fried fish in front of them. Even though they were just bluegills, the smell made Brian salivate.

"Here's to you, Mr. Fisherman," Granny raised her martini glass in a toast, grinning yet again.

Brian raised his water glass, clicked it against Granny's drink, and they smiled at each other while sipping.

Brian had never tasted such good fish in his life.

Darkness fell swiftly on Found Lake that evening. Even though he'd only been there a few days, Brian felt the time passing quickly.

In their wicker chairs, Granny and Brian discussed the Battleground strategy for the next morning. She encouraged him to get back out on the lake and show the walleye what he was made of.

"I will," Brian said, dipping a spoon into a bowl of vanilla ice cream—something he'd still been waiting for since the last day of school. It tasted better than it would've at home.

"You gotta get more exploring done," Granny said, cracking a match to light another cigarette.

"Where did my dad go exploring when he was here?" Brian asked.

"His favorite was the path alongside the lake. Follow the pines down by the lakeshore to the right and you'll find it."

"Is it muddy?" Brian asked, still mourning his destroyed new sneakers in the back of his mind.

"Nah. But be prepared for anything out there." Granny raised her eyebrows playfully.

"Yeah, I've kinda learned that," Brian pointed at his ruined shoes in the corner of the porch.

Granny's laughter echoed over the yard.

After finishing her martini, Granny brought

two decks of cards from the kitchen. She scooted the old wooden table forward, and motioned for Brian to adjust his seat to face her from the other side of the tabletop.

"You like card games?" Granny asked, her tone expectant.

"Yes."

"Of course you do. You're my grandson."

Brian smiled.

"I'm going to teach you the game that we're going to play all summer," she said, her tiny hands bending the card stacks nearly in half as she shuffled them.

This game, it turned out, was double-handed solitaire. Brian loved playing solitaire on his own at home, but never thought he was exceptionally good at it. The first thing Brian learned about playing this game with Granny was that she really, really liked winning.

As they each turned over their cards and placed them down in their columns, furrowing their brows when one couldn't be played, the temperature on the porch seemed to increase, despite the sun having set already.

"Faster!" Granny yelled out, making Brian jump.

Flip, flip, place, flip, "Crap!" Granny's hands would flash like lightning in front of Brian as she slammed cards onto his columns. "Hey!"

"Move it! Move it!" Granny shouted between

bouts of laughter.

After what seemed like three hours pressed against hot coals and Granny's competitive, wild glare, Brian called out in victory. "I have no cards left!"

"Oh, hell!" Granny spat, throwing her remaining cards at Brian's face.

"I won!" Brian clapped his hands down on the teetering little table.

"Oh, hush up," Granny Jane threw another stack of cards into his lap. "Beginner's luck."

They grinned at each other in the darkness for a moment.

"I should've known you'd be good at this game," she grumbled. "You're my grandson."

Brian flashed a wide, toothy sneer at his grandmother, and she launched another wad of cards against his forehead.

Cat poked her head out onto the porch, her eyes wide with concern at the racket that had ruined her nap in the sitting room.

"Don't get too worked up, Granny," Brian teased. "Save some of that energy for the beavers."

"Watch it, boy," Granny raised herself out of her chair. "I got more energy than you could even imagine." Still smiling, she muttered to herself about her cheating grandson as she made herself another martini in the kitchen.

The two enjoyed the crickets and quiet

for a while. Brian reflected on his day on the lake. He wondered if the beavers were on the Battleground, preparing more barriers for he and Granny to destroy the next morning. He enjoyed the feeling of purpose and pride in his chest when he thought about his daily endeavors with Granny. The Lake was already his new home, and he liked defending it.

Granny Jane said goodnight. Brian sat on the porch a while longer, listening to a lone loon crying out on the lake. Cat found her way into Brian's lap and her scratchy purr reminded him of Granny's voice.

Yawning, Brian gathered up the giant cat and carried her up to bed with him. Once his shoes were off and his pajamas were on, Brian sat on the side of his bed. He opened his suitcase and pulled out a few photographs he'd stashed in there before being taken from home.

Gazing down at the picture of him standing, smiling, beside his parents on a picnic they'd taken last summer, an ache in his chest joined the ache in his back and arms. He missed them, he missed home, but less and less every day. The thought of going back was becoming an unpleasant idea.

Turning out the light and pulling the quilt to his chin, Brian decided he'd be fine with staying at Found Lake with Granny for a lot longer than a summer.

Chapter Six

The morning sun slid behind a few clouds as Granny and Brian stood at the dam, inspecting the reinforcements the beavers had built overnight. Brian shook his head in continued disbelief.

The evil beavers had replaced almost the entire dam.

"Granny," Brian said. "How do they fix the whole thing in one night?"

"Persistence," she muttered. "And resilience."

Both of them inhaled deeply, preparing to defend the woods from the beavers once more.

"I'll start on top this time," Granny said, adjusting her waders and heading toward the wall of sticks.

The morning continued in silent dedication to the cause. Brian was thankful that clouds blocked most of the sun. His burns needed a bit of a rest.

No matter how tired they got, they didn't slow or cease their efforts. After they felt satisfied with over half the dam deconstructed, they moved the piles of sticks all the way to the side of the shed beside the cottage.

"Cut off their resources!" Granny yowled, throwing up an exhausted but intent hand. "We've got them now."

Brian was grateful when they finally hung up their waders for the afternoon. Granny decided to go into town for groceries, directing Brian to clean up after their lunch before he went exploring.

«§»

The clouds had turned darker and thicker by the time Brian found the trail alongside the lake. Despite the threat of rain, he plodded on, his eyes tilted up to the tops of the pines.

He fashioned himself a nice walking stick along his way, brushing moss off the handle. Three chipmunks dashed across the dirt path in front of him, one of them stopping to stare at him before trailing its friends into a patch of ferns.

The forest floor was cool and the smell of dense, green leaves followed Brian's nose. A few more chipmunks leapt about the trail. Squirrels chided him from around a bend, and he raised his stick, cawing back at them. He wasn't just a fisherman-in-training at Found Lake—he was a master of the woodlands, too.

The dirt had veins of red clay running through it near the bases of the trees. Every now and then, he bent over to collect pale white stones that shone brightly, even in the cloudy afternoon.

Brian came to an opening in the trees that framed a stretch of the lakeshore. He set the tip of his walking stick firmly into the ground and surveyed the water. A wind sighed up through the cattails below, the scent of cold rain flowing along with it. Brian patted the treasured rocks in his pocket.

A deer was drinking on the water's edge a few hundred feet away. *I'll make a bow and arrow out of sticks next*, Brian decided. *If Granny can live like a pioneer on her own, so can I!*

Carrying on, Brian wondered how long he'd been walking. It was hard to tell what time of day it was with the sun behind ever-darkening storm clouds.

By the time Brian reached the end of the trail and turned to head back to the cottage, it was starting to drizzle. He increased his pace. The air had grown much colder, and he realized that a true master of the woodlands would've planned ahead and probably brought a sweatshirt.

As he trekked, becoming nervous with the growls of thunder, the raindrops became larger. He wiped one off the tip of his nose. The wind whipped at the tops of the pines now, and they swayed, directing Brian toward home.

The sky was now completely black with the storm. He broke into a jog, goosebumps rising on his forearms. Fear rose up in his chest; all of the stories his mother had told him about kids getting struck by lightning while playing out in storms rolled through his mind alongside the thunder. He wondered if his father had ever gotten trapped in a Found Lake thunderstorm; had he been afraid? Or did he remain tough?

The first heavy sheet of rain blew down over the forest, drenching Brian instantly. He abandoned his walking stick (along with the rest of his courage) and lurched into a sprint, his hands shielding his very wide eyes. He was shaking so violently his knees were buckling. The thunder began blending with his heartbeat hammering in his ears.

It felt like years before the cottage came back into view, barely visible through the wall of rain. The lightning and thunder argued loudly with each other now. Brian feared the cracks and rumbles would deafen him.

Rushing up to the house in heavy clothes, Brian saw Granny's old car parked outside.

Brian burst onto the porch, tripping on the

last step on his way through the screen door. Catching himself with his hands, he crawled past the doorway and looked up to find Granny watching him from her wicker chair.

Rain dripped off his hair and into his eyes.

"Adventuring?" Granny asked as he shook the water from his arms.

"Yeah," he exhaled through shivers.

"Towels in the bathroom. Get warm clothes on."

Brian looked up at her, wondering what that edge was in her tone. He thought she would've been laughing at him, but she remained still and cool.

He returned to the porch in dry clothes and socks a few minutes later. "Did you get back before the storm?"

"Yes," she replied over the pounding rain on the porch roof. "I knew the storm was coming. Beat it."

"I guess I should've listened to the forecast on the radio before going hiking." Brian sat down in his wicker chair.

"Yes. You should have. It's dangerous being out there in weather like this. Tornado season, boy."

Brian looked at his feet. *She's mad.*

"I know you're old enough to know that," she continued. "Something could've happened out there. You didn't even have a raincoat. You'll get yourself into quite some trouble out here if you don't use your head, you hear me?"

Brian nodded. He picked at his nails. "Sorry."

"Don't apologize. You may be tough, but real toughness requires brains."

"Yes, ma'am," he whispered.

"Right. Right then." Her gaze returned to the yard filling with puddles. She pulled her blanket tighter around her arms.

They listened to the storm growl fiercely once more and then begin tapering off. Brian didn't say anything more before Granny got up to bang dishes around for dinner.

Third lesson learned at Found Lake: you couldn't be tough if you were dead...or soaking wet and stumbling.

«§»

After breaking down the dam and cracking sticks the next morning, Brian and Granny spent some time in her gardens.

She was no longer angry about the evening before, and Brian was grateful. He loved watching her throw her hands about in the air, describing how to keep soil healthy with eggshells and coffee grounds, and the importance of trimming dead leaves regularly.

A majority of her ranting sounded like a

foreign language to Brian. His mother had plants back at home, but they were just little things she kept in a few pots on the front porch. She even forgot to water them sometimes, and their leaves would brown and lilt.

Side by side, Granny and Brian snipped some dead fern leaves here and there, then dug up some phlox and moved them to the garden she was building on the other side of the house.

"This is much easier with someone else helping," Granny said, brushing dirt off her hands on her old jeans. "We'll move a few bluebells next."

"Your flowers are much nicer and bigger than my mom's," Brian said, scooping at soil with a small shovel.

"Well," Granny tilted her chin, clearly enjoying the compliment, "it must be hard to raise any plants properly in the city."

Brian tried fishing off the dock later that day, but didn't even get a single bite. Maybe the fish had learned that those night crawlers weren't just free floating snacks. Once again, Brian accepted that he needed to have the persistence that the beavers had with his battles that summer. He would catch that walleye; he would clear the dam once and for all; and yes, he would become a pioneer like Granny—not a soaking wet, scared kid.

For the first time that summer, Granny invited a friend over for dinner to meet Brian. His name was Jack.

The first thing Brian noticed when he shook Jack's stubby, callused hand was that he smelled strongly of chewing tobacco—and he was much shorter than most men Brian knew.

"Nice to know ya, Brian," Jack said, releasing Brian's fingers and fishing a tin canister of tobacco out of his red and black flannel breast pocket. "What is your grandmother making us lucky guys for dinner tonight?"

"Beef stew," Brian said, watching Jack wedge a wad of the tobacco under his lower lip. It created a bulge in the side of his face that made his smile wider.

They all gathered around the kitchen table after Jack greeted Granny Jane with a hug and playful jab at her, as always, very curly hair. Even though Jack was short for a man, he still dwarfed Brian's grandmother.

"Wash your hands and sit down, you two," Granny Jane ordered.

Once the stew was ladled into their bowls, they slurped and gnawed at the hearty chunks of beef.

"Catch anything good yet this summer?" Jack asked the two of them.

Granny Jane immediately started hooting and hollering with laughter, and Brian turned down his red face.

"Not yet," Brian grumbled.

"Ah, you will," Jack said. "We've caught some great ones out here. Your grandmother holds the record for biggest fish. A northern pike. Never seen anything like it. It was bigger than her."

Brian cracked a smile as Granny brushed off the (backhanded) compliment with her hand. "Rubbish. Brian will catch something twice as big by the end of the summer."

Once Brian and Jack finished the dishes for Granny, who sat peacefully with a cigarette and martini in the sitting room, they all retreated to the screened porch to listen to the radio and crickets.

"You know, Jack," Granny Jane mentioned, "Brian is quite good at double-handed solitaire."

"Well, if you taught him, of course he is." Jack chortled.

"We'll start playing after I get another gin," Granny Jane decided.

Brian spooned more ice cream into his mouth, wondering how much more intense the game would be with another player. Hopefully Granny wouldn't find anything heavier than cards to throw at them…

When Granny returned with a freshly filled martini, Jack shuffled the massive stack of worn, torn cards. Cat had made her way onto the porch, as usual, but had a wary look about her—she knew it wouldn't be quiet for long.

"I'm gonna get you this time, boy," Granny Jane's eyes narrowed on Brian.

Feeling the porch heat up already, Brian replied, "That's what you think."

"Ah," Granny raised an eyebrow. "We'll see."

Through their table talk, Jack finished shuffling and divvied out everyone's decks. They placed their cards in preparation, and then Granny shouted, "On your marks!"

In a split second, Brian and Granny had fired away. Doling, dishing, swiping, and nabbing, the two stacked their cards, tossed cards toward the other player, and heckled each other.

"You're falling behind!" Brian teased Granny.

"Watch your cards, boy!" she snapped.

They swapped decks, tossed more cards over, and hammered each one as quickly as possible into its designated spot. Through the fire, Brian didn't notice at all that Jack was completely silent and composed. He was much more worried about beating his grandmother a second time.

"You're done for!" Granny screeched, shaking the table as she slammed down two more cards.

"Yeah, right!" cried Brian.

A series of more cards flickered across the table, and Brian and Granny cussed under their breath as their stacks got smaller and smaller.

Suddenly, Jack said, "Done."

Even the crickets stopped chirping.

"What?" Granny barked.

"Done." Jack repeated. "I've finished." It was the only thing he'd said the entire game.

"You can't be done!" Brian exclaimed.

They looked down at the cards neatly placed in front of Jack, and to their great horror, he had indeed beaten both of them.

"Gah, hell!" snarled Granny. "Unbelievable!"

Brian was gaping again. This time, he didn't try to close his mouth.

"Good game," Jack beamed, stuffing another heap of tobacco under his lip.

"I..." Brian groaned. "Come on!"

After the shock wore off a bit, Granny proposed they play again.

Jack won the next game, too, silently, calmly, and smugly.

Granny slammed her fist on the table. "What the heck are you doing? You're cheating!"

"I'm not cheating, Jane," he laughed.

The fact that Jack found this terrible situation funny turned Granny's and Brian's faces to stone.

"That's funny?!" snapped Granny.

"Yeah, that's funny?" Brian echoed.

"You must be related to her," Jack said to Brian, nodding toward Granny Jane. "Competition in the blood, these two!"

"AGAIN!" screamed Granny.

The third round ended the same way the first two had, except this time the small wooden table found itself thrown across the screen porch. Granny was much stronger than she looked.

The fireflies were out amongst the pine trees now, and after ten minutes of fuming that turned to giggling and then bouts of laughter, Cat decided to come out from the bathroom where she had been hiding from the noise.

Granny had another martini, and she blew smoke toward the ceiling as she patted Cat's head. Jack had his feet up now, looking unusually comfortable for being in a wicker chair. Brian had decided to eat his frustrations and had another bowl of ice cream in his lap.

"Great dinner, Jane," Jack said. "Thanks."

"Anytime, cheater," Granny Jane retorted.

Laughter broke out again.

They listened to the radio for an hour, soaking in the owl hoots from the edge of the yard. Jack fell asleep in his wicker chair, and Granny studied the yard for ages, lost in deep thought.

Brian found himself dozing off in his chair, too, while thinking about how many times he'd beat his friends at double-handed solitaire once he taught them how to play. He still couldn't believe Jack—who hadn't even said a word during the game!—had won every single round.

Fourth lesson learned at Found Lake: being loud didn't always make you the victor.

«§»

The days began blending together as July arrived. Every morning was spent at the Battleground, and the afternoons were filled with hours of hiking, fishing, exploring, and always olive loaf sandwiches for lunch.

Evenings were cards, baseball games on the radio, pets for Cat, and Jack's bulging, smiley cheeks when he stopped by.

Brian still hadn't had his rematch with the walleye, but he knew he'd find that fish before long. His determination grew with each passing day.

The middays grew hotter and hotter, even when a rainstorm would bluster through and break the heat every now and then. Brian's ever-present sunburns had turned into a brown, freckled tan.

Cat grew fatter and fatter. Granny had started treating her to snips of meat from dinner in hopes her kittens would be born strong. Baby squirrels had been born in the backyard, too.

Brian hadn't once called home. He was already home.

"You know, Granny," Brian said one afternoon as the two were reading on the porch, "you never go out on your motor boat."

"Oh, that thing." Granny Jane snorted. "It's a hunk of junk. It still works, but I prefer the canoe—just like I bet you do."

"Well, sure," Brian said, setting down his comic book, "but don't you wanna go out on it at all this summer?"

"Hmm." Granny didn't take her eyes off her newspaper. "I guess we could take it out once. You have to learn to waterski, after all."

"What?" Brian blinked.

"Waterskiing. I have to teach you to waterski."

Again, Brian's jaw dropped, of course, just when he thought Granny Jane couldn't surprise him anymore. "I have no idea how to waterski! You have skis? Can *you* waterski?"

"Of course I can, boy."

He stared at her. She still didn't look up, but now she was grinning into her paper.

"Is it dangerous?" Brian asked.

"What do you think?" she leered at him.

A few hours later, Brian and Granny had dug the wooden skis out of the shed and down to the dock. Granny jangled the keys in her hands as Brian set the skis in the back of the boat. He'd only been on a motorboat once before—and his palms were sweaty with excitement, of course.

The seats were damp and musty from being out in the rain and sun the whole summer, but they were worn and comfortable. Granny stuck the keys in the ignition and turned them. After a wet churning and grumble, the motor started.

"Can't believe this old thing still runs," she scoffed.

Brian untied the boat from the pier and, with a burp of gassy smoke, they were heading out onto Found Lake.

Once they had idled out into the middle of the lake, Granny turned down the engine. "All right, get down to your trunks and hop in."

"What?" Brian looked around, as if the lake could clear his confusion for him. "I just...jump in?"

"I bought you a life jacket for skiing last time I was in town," Granny said, yanking a bright orange vest up from beside the driver's seat. "I know you can swim, but if ya knock your head, you're fish food." She tossed the vest to her grandson.

Hesitantly, Brian took off his T-shirt and shoes. He strapped on the vest. "When do I put on the skis?" he asked.

"Jump in first, boy," Granny Jane said.

"Jump? Just...jump?" Brian asked.

"You got it."

Brian tiptoed to the back of the boat, gingerly stepped up onto the back seat, held his breath, and sprung into the water. Shocked and freezing, he sucked in air once he reached the surface. He floated there for a moment, careful to avoid the smoky motor.

Granny stepped toward the back of the boat, her little curly head now visible to Brian down in the water. She threw a long, red rope into the water. "Grab the handle," she hollered.

Brian was shaking from a heavy combination of fear and the chilled water. He stretched out his fingers and grasped the hard plastic triangle handle, gripping it tightly.

Granny slid the skis down into the water to him one by one. They floated on the lake's surface.

"Slip those feet into the skis, and then you're set to go," she said.

Bobbling about the water awkwardly, the lifejacket shoved up snuggly under his chin, Brian shoved his feet into the boots on the tops of the skis.

"Now," Granny instructed, "you're gonna put the skis out in front of you, tips to the sky. Keep your legs straight, but bend your knees to start with. Let the boat pull you up—don't try and stand up too quick, or you'll face-plant! Keep your balance."

"Granny, I have no idea what I'm doing," Brian whined, the shaking traveling to his teeth.

"Boy!" Granny hollered as she returned to the

driver's seat, "there's nothing to worry about. Let the boat do all the work; don't fight it."

Before Brian knew it, the motor was gurgling and spitting smoke again, and Granny hit the gas.

The rope attached to the back of the motorboat snapped taut, and Brian was suddenly underwater, choking and swallowing. *I'm going to drown!*

His rock solid grip on the handle loosened slightly when the rope went slack and he resurfaced, gasping and coughing. Through watery eyes, he saw Granny on the boat, flailing her hands at him.

"Keep your skis in front of you and your arms straight, boy!" she shouted.

"I'm trying!" Brian yelled, spitting water.

"Don't try!" she howled. "Do!"

Brian sighed, overwhelmed. Was she trying to kill him?

"Here we go again!" he heard from the boat.

The engine turned, and Granny took off yet again.

Brian watched the rope disappear between his skis, snap tight, and the water started funneling about his feet as he was pulled forward. He slowly sat up as the boat pulled him from the water, sensing the vibrating pressure. Every part of him wanted to give up, but he remained resilient. He would hold on.

The first thing he noticed as he rose out of the water was how cold his bottom was, soaking with his bathing shorts flapping.

The wind pushed at his eyes, and he squinted as he straightened his legs more and more. He was almost standing! He was moving! He was gliding on top of the water!

His knees buckled for a second, but he caught himself and, clenching every muscle in his body, he centered himself on top of the skis. Each bit of wake he hit from the boat bobbled him atop the skis, but cementing his grip on the handle, he stabled himself.

He thought he heard Granny Jane hooting from the boat and he watched her tiny fists wave above her head victoriously.

The muscles in his arms started screaming only after a short while, but he held on. Once he'd gotten used to standing atop the water with the wind whipping at him, he let himself lean a bit to each side, watching the water spray off the edges of the skis.

Even though his arms and legs were starting to cry out in pain, too, Brian gazed around and soaked in the view. The pine trees flew by; the sky was open and blue. The eagle that lived on the side of the lake flew overhead, barely impressed with Brian's fantastic feat.

After another circle, the wind howling even louder now in Brian's ears, he released the handle and let himself sink into the water. His muscles instantly sighed with relief.

Brian floated at the surface and watched Granny Jane slow the motor and circle around to get him.

"Fantastic, boy!" she hollered from the boat. "Fantastic! Great first round."

"Granny," Brian wailed, "my arms and legs are killing me!"

"Get used to it!" she barked.

He couldn't help but laugh. The relief traveled from his legs to his tight chest and dizzy head.

Once the smile reached his face, he couldn't get rid of it. Skiing was fun!

He yanked his feet out of the skis and floated with them over to the back of the motorboat.

Granny helped him reel the rope back up into the boat, took the skis from him, and his arms and knees shook from fatigue as he climbed back up.

"That was just great," Granny beamed. "You're definitely my grandson!"

Brian wrapped his towel tightly around his shoulders. He still smiled through chattering teeth.

"Get that vest off, it'll keep you cold," Granny laughed. She unstrapped him and he rewrapped the towel around himself.

She drove slowly back to the dock, and Brian found the strength to hop out and tie up their chugging vessel.

"The boat made it!" Brian said.

"It wasn't the boat I was worried about!" Granny crowed.

They gathered up their gear. Granny carried the skis back up, grinning to herself as she watched Brian's shaking legs.

The adrenaline was still pumping through Brian when they entered the cottage, and Granny instructed him to go upstairs and get in warm clothes. "And take a shower, too," she said. "Don't need to stink any more like lake than you already do."

They had a victory dinner of meatloaf that night. Brian felt clean and warm in his pajamas at the kitchen table. His legs still hurt, but the hot meatloaf filling his belly was helping.

Later, they enjoyed a baseball game on the radio, Granny yelling about the score, and Brian grinning with amusement at her passion. Brian was too full from his third helping of meatloaf to have any ice cream for dessert.

During a commercial break, Granny looked over the rim of her martini glass. "Where the heck is that cat?" she grumbled.

Brian realized he hadn't seen Cat once since they returned from their skiing adventure down at the lake. He started looking around, too.

"I haven't seen her," he said, getting out of his wicker chair and gazing into the kitchen.

"Bah, she's around," Granny resigned to remaining in her seat. "Probably just being her fat and lazy self."

After the baseball game ended, Brian stretched and yawned. "I'm really tired, Granny. I'm going to bed."

"You'll sleep well tonight." she said. "Get ready for another go around the lake tomorrow!"

"Okay," Brian laughed. Granny laughed in return. For a moment, he thought he saw a look of pride flash across her face.

Brian made his way up the stairs and into his little bedroom. Holding himself against the candy-striped pole, he pulled his socks off and tossed them into the pile of laundry in the corner.

The socks landed amongst the shirts, and suddenly Brian heard a soft mew.

He squinted in the dim light cast from the lamp on his dresser. "Cat?" he whispered.

Leaning over the pile of clothes, he saw Cat curled up, one of the socks on top of her head. She was twice the size she was the day before!... and what were those little brown patches on her?...

Brian gasped. Cat had five kittens snuggled against her belly!

"Cat! You're a mom!" he said. He pulled the sock off of her face and pet her head. There were two gray kittens, the same color as their mother, and then one red one beside two brown ones.

Brian grabbed an extra quilt off his bed and wrapped Cat and her kittens in a cozy nest. He sat and watched them for a while in the quiet. One of the kittens squeaked. Cat looked up to check on it, determined all was well, and laid down her tired head to rest.

Smiling, Brian laid down, too, and was asleep before his head hit the pillow.

Chapter Seven

After a few more weeks, Brian's legs didn't even shake anymore when he hopped back into the boat after skiing.

There were sunflowers reaching all the way up to the bottoms of the cottage windows now. Granny liked to gather the seeds off the ground in the evenings before dinner. "They'll be planted next spring," she said.

The Beaver Dam Battleground continued to gain and lose its dam on a daily basis. Every move Granny and Brian made was immediately countered by the beavers. The contention and determination remained, but Brian was starting to really wonder if it was a practical activity. Granted, that may have been because all he really wanted to do was ski and fish.

He'd built a fort out of extra dam sticks in a wooded nook along the lake trail. He had a hideaway inside the farmhouse and outside.

Some chipmunks hid in his fort at night every now and then, and he'd laugh every time they scampered out from between the logs when he approached it in the afternoons.

Granny was proud to be grandmother to not just Brian, but now the five little kittens. They had opened their eyes and could waddle around and nip at Cat's ears while she was trying to nap. They would mew softly at night, and the sound was comforting to Brian while he drifted off to sleep.

Brian had gotten even better at double-handed solitaire, but Granny Jane had been on a major winning streak that week. He hadn't beaten her in six days. Jack had been away on a fishing trip, and it gave the two of them the chance to finally duel it out in the evenings without being squashed by him every time.

Brian was getting better at fishing, too. Although he'd not seen anything bigger than a baby smallmouth bass on the end of his line, he was able to put a fish dinner on the table several times a week—and Granny had taught him how to cook the fish, too.

Granny was taking her shift on top of the dam one unusually hot morning. She was yanking hard at a long, thick stick, cussing at it while struggling to keep her balance. Brian was by the river's edge, breaking the bigger wood into pieces with his shoes.

After snapping a few smaller sticks in half, he sighed. He stopped and looked up at his grandmother. She continued her rampage on the beaver's home.

"Granny," Brian said.

She didn't respond; she grunted and kicked at the stick she couldn't dislodge.

"Granny," Brian repeated.

She kept at it, completely ignoring him.

"Granny!" he yelled.

"What on earth do you want, boy?" Granny shot back.

Pausing and sighing again, Brian itched the side of his head, his hair warm from the sunlight. "What are we doing this for?"

"I already told you," Granny kept pulling at the stick, "we have to stop the beavers from destroying the land."

"But..." Brian looked up at the sky and around them. "They're...they're just doing what beavers do, aren't they?"

"So what?" Granny hollered. "The trees are dying."

"The trees are okay," Brian motioned around them with his hand. "They're still here, even though the dam's been here the whole time."

"We can't give up now, boy. We've almost got 'em." Granny growled.

"But they're just trying to protect their home, just like we are."

Granny stopped suddenly. She released her grip on the bothersome stick.

"I mean," Brain continued, clearing his throat, "why do they just keep building the dam back up, over and over?"

She furrowed her brow, thinking, and quietly replied, "To save their home."

Brian dropped the last stick in his hand. "I guess we're just like the beavers. And the beavers are just like us."

Granny Jane straightened her back, placed her fists on her hips, and stared out over the swamp for a long while. Brian watched her scan the bog, mulling things over in her mind.

She sighed. She hobbled down from the dam, waded back to the mud, and shook her head. Looking Brian in the eye, she said, "I think it's time to head back."

Brian truly understood resilience then. That was the last time Brian went to the dam that summer.

The lily pads had grown extra thick in the past

few weeks, and it took Brian more time than usual to paddle out to his favorite fishing spot. The sun was high and shining, and the breeze was gentle.

After casting out his crawler, Brian put his feet up on the side of the canoe and leaned back onto its nose. The eagle was watching, as usual. *He's not gonna get any handouts from me*, Brian laughed to himself.

The summer had eased into the heart of August by then. Jack had returned home from his fishing trip, and Brian hoped he would come over soon so that they could spar with cards again. Brian had improved and really wanted to try his luck against the reigning champion.

He closed his eyes and watched the red backs of his eyelids. The water lapped up against the bottom of the boat. He thought about how happy the beavers would be about the war ending. Brian knew he was pretty happy about it; they'd spent so much time tearing things down, fighting against something that was so strangely similar, familiar. He would not have gotten to spend as much time talking to Granny Jane, though, had they not visited the Beaver Dam Battleground so much that summer.

Brian heard the fishing pole knock against the side of the canoe, and his eyes bolted open. Sure enough, his bobber was jumping about in the water.

He sat up, squared his feet, and watched. He reeled in slightly to tease the fish into taking the hook. There was stillness for a moment, and when Brian looked back up at his bobber, it had completely disappeared.

"All right!" he said and started reeling. The line was much, much harder to get in this time—

was he caught on some weeds? Or a log? It was barely coming in at all!

The bobber was still nowhere to be found. How deep had it gone? What was on the line?

Reeling harder and harder, Brian pulled up on the rod and his eyes widened at how much it bent. It looked like it might break.

He reached out and quickly snatched the line with his hand. Bracing the pole, he reeled with his right hand, and pulled the line closer intermittently with his left. Slowly but surely, he felt whatever was on the end of the line fighting back stronger.

The battle raged on, but Brian knew that he had to be patient. He wasn't going to bring it in too quickly for fear of losing his catch—or the giant stick that was on the end of his line.

The fighting slowed a bit, but the line still darted back and forth in the water. He was able to reel a little easier now, and then he caught sight of the bobber. It was nearing the boat, getting closer to the surface of the water.

The pole kept bending, even though he was trying to hold the line, and he prayed it wouldn't snap.

Suddenly, the bobber burst out of the water with a splash, and he snatched the line with both hands, the pole toppling over to the side in the boat. He pulled up on the line, and...

It was the walleye!

Thrashing violently, the giant fish gasped in the air, its scales shining. The hook was deep, and Brian cried out in excitement.

The fish flexed its spiky fins, the sunshine turning it a greenish gold color. Brian lifted the line higher and lowered the incredibly heavy fish into the bottom of the boat.

He heard a hoot echo over the lake all the way from the dock. There was Granny, doing a victory dance on the pier. She'd seen him catch it!

His face ached from grinning. He stood, trying to not tip the boat with excitement, looking down at that epic fish. It flopped about the bottom of the canoe, and after placing a foot on its tail to still it, Brian used a pair of needle-nose pliers to dislodge the hook. The fish was over a foot long. He couldn't believe it.

"We meet again, walleye!" he cheered. Granny echoed him from the shoreline.

Brian grabbed his wire underwater cage and carefully nudged the walleye into it, securing the top of it closed with a piece of twine he grabbed from his pocket.

He'd never paddled so quickly before in his life.

Granny rushed to the edge of the dock and tied up the canoe.

"You got him!" she yelled. "I told you you'd get him eventually!"

"I know! I know!" Brian teetered out of the canoe, and once his feet were solidly on the dock, he raised the wire cage from the water. The mighty walleye tossed about in the bottom of the cage, its eyes wide and unblinking.

"*Now* we're going to eat like kings," Granny laughed. "Congratulations, boy!"

Brian danced in place on the dock. One of his biggest battles on Found Lake had been won.

"Grab him and come on up to the cottage," Granny smiled. "It's time to eat some walleye!"

Granny cleaned the walleye after measuring him. "Fifteen inches," she said. "That's one heck of a fish. We won't be able to eat all of it. I'll save some for Jack."

Brian sat victoriously at the kitchen table, still sweaty from the thrill of his becoming a master fisherman. He was truly proud of himself, and it showed in the way he puffed out his chest whenever Granny complimented him.

"You come here and fry him up, boy," Granny said, poking the spatula in his direction. "He's yours to cook."

Flipping the fish in the pan the way Granny had taught him, Brian triumphantly breathed in the scent of the cooking filet. The pan fish he'd reeled in all throughout that summer had been fine, but this was going to be something else entirely.

Granny Jane chopped up some potatoes and fried them on the stovetop beside Brian. The smile was still plastered on his face, and he wasn't sure it would ever go away.

They set the table, Granny made herself a martini, and as they seated themselves, she made a toast to Brian.

"To the master fisherman of Found Lake," she smirked, her glass held high.

Brian raised his water glass, and then took a big, happy gulp. The first bite of the walleye was enough to make him close his eyes, sigh deeply, and clap his hands a few times.

Granny cleaned her plate way before Brian did. "Best fish I've ever eaten," she burped, patting at her stomach. "Great work."

Brian was impressed with how much fish he was able to eat, and there was still so much more now wrapped and sitting in the refrigerator.

Granny clashed and banged dishes around in the sink, having offered to be on cleaning duty for that evening to reward Brian. She'd put a piece of walleye on a plate for Cat and set it on the kitchen floor. Brian made his bowl of ice cream and kicked up his feet in his wicker chair on the porch.

Granny filled her martini glass and took her seat beside him on the porch. The house still smelled deliciously of cooked fish. He was already excited to have some for breakfast the next morning.

The two basked in the glow of the setting sun. The loons were out and singing already.

"Wanna play cards tonight?" Brian asked, slurping on his ice cream spoon.

"Ah, sure," Granny said. "I'm not gonna let you win just because you're the fishing master, though."

Brian laughed. "Sure, whatever you say."

Cat wandered out onto the porch, licking her lips to not waste any little bits of fish that might be left on her whiskers.

"She enjoyed it, too," Granny said.

Granny turned on the radio, but neither of them really paid much attention to it.

Suddenly, the phone rang in the kitchen. Granny ignored it. The event of a phone call was extremely rare at the cottage, and he looked at her with anticipation.

"Are you going to get that?" he asked.

"Nah. I spent all that blasted money on an answering machine, let it do its job."

The ringing stopped and a message was recorded.

Brian took a few more bites of ice cream. Cat rolled about the carpet, as usual, but then retreated back into the house to check on her kittens. Hopefully they hadn't waddled and tumbled too far from their nest in Brian's bedroom.

Granny snubbed out her cigarette in the dish on the table, stood up, and shuffled to the kitchen. Brian listened to her making another martini, and then she pressed a button on the answering machine. The message on the recording was quiet, but Brian immediately recognized that it was his father's voice.

He turned around in his seat. He couldn't make out what his dad was saying, so he watched Granny instead. She showed no change in demeanor. The message ended, she picked up her filled glass, and she walked back out onto the porch.

"Was that my dad?" Brian asked.

"Yes." she eased into her chair, her face still.

"What'd he say?"

"Oh, nothing. Nothing to worry about."

"But Dad never calls." Brian insisted.

"It's nothing, boy." Granny Jane grunted. "We'll talk about it tomorrow."

Brian didn't move his eyes from her, a weird tingling starting in the pit of his stomach. He felt a rush of those feelings again...the feelings he'd forgotten about when he arrived at Found Lake. He didn't like the way it made the back of his neck sweat.

"It's just..." Granny started again, pursing her lips, "your dad called, yes, and he told me that it's time for you to...go home."

"No." Brian jumped out of his wicker chair.

"No!"

"What do you mean, 'no'?" Granny's eyes met his. "You have school starting again soon. Things have calmed down at home. The summer's gonna be over soon."

"No, Granny!" Brian shouted.

"Lower your voice!" she hit her hand against her thigh. "What's wrong with you? Of course you have to go back for school."

"I don't want to go back there, to…that place. It's not my home anymore. I can go to school up here."

"Don't be ridiculous," Granny laughed.

Brian clenched his fists and felt his throat closing up. "I…" he choked, "I'm not going back. I won't do it!"

"Brian, you're going back home whether you like it or not." Granny set down her glass on the table.

He glared at her. For the first time that summer, he was angry with his Granny Jane. His hands were shaking and he couldn't stop the burning of tears in his eyes.

"I won't do it." he snapped.

She shook her head. She looked away from him, turned the radio back up, and picked up her martini glass again. "I know you don't want to. But you're going home. No matter what. Just because you don't want to go doesn't mean you don't have to. You can't avoid your problems."

"I won't go!" he repeated. A tear had made its way down to his chin.

"You will. You must. You're a grownup now. You have to face your fears and do things you don't like sometimes."

He rubbed his cheek with his fist. "I don't have to."

"I won't say it again, boy," she growled, the bear purr more than present in her voice. "You've faced your fears all summer—you didn't run away when I made you put those skis on, did you? You faced a thunderstorm that nearly drowned ya. You helped Cat raise five kittens. You didn't run away or give up when you didn't catch that walleye, right?"

Brian bit down hard on his lip. Everything in his body was telling him to run away now— regardless of what Granny Jane was saying. Another tear rolled down his cheek.

"Your family needs you, too. I can't have you all to myself forever." Granny sipped her drink calmly.

"You're the only family I want. They don't care about me—they only care about themselves," Brian mumbled, his words getting caught in his throat.

"Don't you dare say that about your parents; they love you more than anything in the world. They didn't try to hurt you. Stop being selfish. You know better."

Brian clenched his jaw and exhaled. "It's not fair."

"Life isn't fair, Brian." Granny Jane narrowed her eyes on him. "Found Lake should've taught you that. Things can be scary, or difficult, or tiring. But you have to protect your home, and take care of those you love. Just like a beaver."

He wiped away another tear and sat down again. All he wanted to do was hug Granny, but he was shaking too much to stand.

Granny sighed. "And Found Lake isn't your only home. You have to be there for your family. You can't give up or stop being resilient, no matter what."

"But, Granny..." Brian held his face in his hands.

"Nope. You know it's true. And stop your worrying and bellyaching," she said with a small smile. "You got nothing to fret about. Because no matter what, no matter what you have to face when you get back home...you will always have yourself, and you will always have Found Lake."

Chapter Eight

Brian rose from his bed well before sunrise the next morning. He couldn't sleep—not while knowing that he had limited time at Found Lake left.

He walked quietly throughout the cottage, careful to not disturb Granny and Cat with her kittens. On the porch, he slid on his worn old sneakers and walked out into the yard. The lingering night held the air cold and still, dew gathering on the grass and pine needles.

Brian made his way down to the dock and sat on the cracked wooden bench. The moon had sunk just below the tops of the pines, and the nearing sunrise glowed from across the other side of the lake.

As much as he wanted to avoid it, the events of the night before pressed on his mind. Granny Jane's words repeated in his head. He wanted to be resilient for her—he wanted to be the strong grandson that she always claimed he was. The urge to run was overwhelming.

He couldn't imagine going home now...now that he had Found Lake...now that he had found himself...now that he had Granny. Returning to the confusion and crying parents and stomachaches and dizziness seemed impossible.

More tears escaped his eyes. The cattails caught a breeze and swayed, the lake grass rustled; he took them in and let it fill his mind for a while. If he had no choice about going back, which seemed to be the way of it, he could always retreat back into these memories. His gut told him that he'd need to hold on to his moments at Found Lake a lot in the coming weeks, months... years.

Two loons floated by, not even noticing him in the darkness. Even though the sunlight was so dim, the white bands around their necks and red eyes seemed to glow.

Once the sun had risen over the trees and the eagle had left his perch, Brian made his way back up to the cottage to see if his Granny Jane was up and waging war on breakfast.

Brian and Granny Jane spent the last few days of their first summer together as though nothing had changed. They went fishing in the birch canoe, put the last touches on the gardens, played cards, and skied. Brian fashioned a big box with blankets and little toys for the kittens to enjoy while he was gone.

On his last visit to his fort alongside the lake trail, Brian reinforced the makeshift shelter with heavier sticks and extra twine. He picked patches of moss and laid them on the floor of the hideout for the chipmunks to sleep on.

Granny Jane and Brian didn't speak of his impending departure. They both understood what was needed and would happen; it was more important to both of them that they enjoy their last bits of time together. Brian noticed that Granny made a point to hug him once each day before the blue grumbling Cadillac would be back to take him away.

Sitting on the screen porch on their last night, Granny with her martini and Brian with his bowl of ice cream, they both felt August begin sighing into September. The heat had mostly broken for the season, and fall was settling in. The leaves smelled heavier on the wind, the soil denser and cooler.

Fifth lesson learned at Found Lake: resilient pioneers could adapt to the changing seasons—and everything else that came their way.

"What a lovely summer," Granny sighed, puffing smoke to the ceiling.

"The best summer." Brian nodded, patting Cat in his lap.

Granny lifted her martini, Brian lifted his water glass, and they toasted.

«§»

The blue grumbling Cadillac was running in the driveway when Brian lugged his suitcase down the porch steps.

"Hello again, young man," Uncle Phil said from the open passenger-side door. Brian waved.

Granny stood next to Uncle Phil, her arms crossed, having a small conversation. When she saw Brian come outside, she instantly came to him, grabbed up his suitcase, and started hauling it to the trunk of the car, the same lurching way she'd done when Brian had arrived at Found Lake.

Brian walked alongside her and helped pull the luggage. They both lifted the suitcase into the trunk, and they both closed the trunk together.

The moment the trunk slammed shut, Brian felt his throat closing, trying to hold down crying.

"Good to see ya, Granny," Uncle Phil called and then lumbered into the driver's seat, signaling that it was already time to go.

Brian closed his eyes, afraid to look at

Granny. He didn't have to open his eyes to know how she felt. Her tiny arms wrapped around him, squeezed him, her curly little head on his shoulder.

He held her tightly, breathing in the perfect combination of cigarettes in her hair and the pines above them.

"You're resilient. You're my grandson." Granny said into his shirt.

He smiled, his vision becoming blurry.

"You will always have you. You will always have Found Lake." she released him, squeezed his hand gently, and then led him by the shoulders into the car.

As the blue Cadillac pulled out of the driveway, Brian turned around to wave to Granny through the back window.

Granny stood amongst the pine cones and flowers, waving back with one hand. Her tiny frame started to shrink as they drove farther toward Kleppe road. Small and curly-headed, Granny Jane stood like a giant—a pioneer of the forest.

The car turned onto the road and the cottage and Granny vanished. Brian turned back around in his seat and set his gaze on the road ahead of them, his breathing steady. He was a master fisherman, a storm chaser, an adventurer of the north woods. He would not run.

Sixth lesson learned at Found Lake: the most unfamiliar of places and people could quickly make you the most familiar with yourself.

Brian was standing at the living room window of his lake house again. Another day on the lake was coming to a close in northern Wisconsin. The sun was setting across the water, golden and blazing.

He'd spent the day fishing and hiking with his children, and they'd eaten the walleye his son had caught for dinner. His wife was finishing up with the last of the dishes in the kitchen, and the kids were getting their pajamas on before they had their nightly bowls of vanilla ice cream.

His eyes following a pair of eagles gliding over the treetops, Brian thought about the countless sunsets he and Granny Jane had spent together in those woods...the hours of cards, walking, planting flowers, skiing, petting Cat. Talking, but enjoying each other's quiet.

The children shuffled into the living room in their slippers, already dipping their spoons into their ice cream bowls.

"Daddy," his daughter said, plopping herself into the old wicker armchair Brian had sat in countless evenings at Found Lake, "tell us another story about Granny Jane."

Brian smiled at the glass of the window, closed his eyes, and turned around. He sat in Granny's wicker armchair beside his daughter and pulled his son into his lap. His wife came into the living room and smiled at them.

"Well," Brian smiled, "one summer, Granny Jane and I discovered how much like beavers we are."

The sun disappeared and the crickets sang to the dancing fireflies outside. A loon wailed from the other side of the lake, saying goodnight.

Some things about the woods never changed.

There would always be their Found Lake.

About the Author:
Brian Kludt

Nationally renowned business leader, coach, and speaker, Brian Kludt, has earned a reputation as a visionary in helping others to live a life with intention and purpose. His dream to share these cherished values begins with sharing his coming-of-age lessons learned in his first book, *Found Lake*. Brian, his wife Kathy, and their three children, Jake, Hannah, and Holly, continue to "pay it forward," creating and sharing transformational experiences for family and friends in their northern Wisconsin lake home.

About the Co-Author:
RaeAnne Marie Scargall

RaeAnne Marie Scargall, a creative writing and poetics student of Boulder, Colorado's Naropa University and graduate of the University of Wisconsin-Whitewater, specializes in editing, poetry, creative nonfiction, and fiction. She has been thrilled to create her first full-length piece of children's literature alongside Brian Kludt with *Found Lake*. RaeAnne looks forward to doing more in children's literature, alongside continuing her nonstop editing and writing career in adult literature.

About the Illustrator:
SPENSER BOWER

Spenser Bower is a graduate at the art charter high school, Kettle Moraine Perform. He has received multiple pre-merit art scholarships across the U.S., including in prestigious schools such as Milwaukee Institute of Art and Design (MIAD) and Savannah College of Art and Design (SCAD). He sculpted an exhibit for Milwaukee Art Museum's sculpture exhibit and has been presenting art shows for years. Artistically mature beyond his years, it's no surprise that his award-winning work has already been recognized by top art organizations. Spenser enjoys the creative flexibility of book collaboration, while choosing his career path alongside a loving family.